Snake Eyes

A HORROR SHORT STORY COLLECTION

HUNTER EVANS

Snake

Eyes

HUNTER EVANS

Snake Eyes

The middle-aged gentleman stared longingly at his reflection, seemingly noticing the wrinkles around his eyes for the first time. As he dabbed flesh-colored concealer here and there, a young man walked up behind him, interrupting his preparations for taking the stage for the last time in his long career as a world-renowned botany professor.

"I'm sorry to interrupt, sir, but someone is here to—"

"Do you not see I'm in the middle of doing something important, young man?" the professor interrupted. "Whoever it is, well, they're just going to have to wait."

"He says it's urgent, sir," he responded in a much-softer voice, lowering his head in submission.

Before the professor had a chance to open his

mouth to insult the young man, an intern with a clipboard came rushing toward him. "They're about to announce you, sir, if you'll come this way."

The professor turned away from the strange young man and laughed, taking one last look at his reflection. As he stood up, he towered over the young man and almost seemed to sparkle from every crisp angle of his well-tailored tuxedo. The intern led the way with the professor following him, and the young man watched him walk out of his sight.

Waiting by the side of the stage, the bored expression on the professor's face suddenly changed when he heard his name called. He painted a picture-perfect smile on his face, walked out onto the stage, and looked out at the packed crowd. They cheered and celebrated his existence—he couldn't get enough of their adoration.

"Thank you, thank you, ladies and gentlemen. Thank you for coming—and thank you for that warm welcome." He paused and waited for the cheering to stop again. When it did, the audience seemed to wait on the edge of their seats for the professor to speak as the lights dimmed, and two pictures were displayed on the big screen.

"We're here to celebrate David Hestle and William Danforth, the two grad students who are receiving an enormous honor from the Committee for Scientific Discoveries tonight."

Out of the corner of his eye, the professor saw a monster of a human being limp through the doors of the auditorium. As the light peered through the opened door, he could barely make out a misshapen body that made the professor think that he was, in fact, a monster. He took a sharp breath in and looked back to his expectant audience.

"Uh . . . but, before we bring William and David to the stage, I want to read a little bit from the letter they received from the committee." The professor pulled out a crisp piece of paper with a typed letter that filled the page.

"The committee was impressed with your research paper outlining your innovative grafting technique that resulted in the *theobroma cacao* plant requiring 75% less water than average. We feel this could make a substantial beneficial change to cacao farming worldwide, and we hail you both as innovators par excellence."

The professor put aside the letter and continued his speech: "As I stand in front of you all this evening, Mr. Hestle and Mr. Danforth are returning from their all-expenses-paid trip to the Amazon—courtesy of a generous grant from the Committee for Scientific Discoveries. They've also been awarded a $100,000 grant each for their continued research."

The professor stopped speaking, and his face turned as white as a sheet as he listened to someone speaking to him through his earpiece. "Are you sure?" he whispered.

"Ladies and gentlemen, I apologize for the interruption, but I've just been informed that William Danforth has been presumed dead and did not return from the trip to the Amazon." He stopped and looked nervously at the audience, who let out a symphony of oohs and ahhs at this devastating news.

Then the professor regained his composure and continued, "But William's partner, David Hestle, should be arriving on stage any second now to speak to you all about their trip."

Everyone in the audience seemed confused as to how to respond to the news of William's death. Some stood and cheered the achievements of David and William, while the others just sat in their seats, still shocked to hear about the tragedy. The professor looked off stage at two of the interns arguing quietly. He walked over to them to find out what was going on. "Is Mr. Hestle here yet??" he demanded.

Both the interns looked at each other, then back to the professor. "We don't know, sir," one of them said. "Nobody has seen or heard from him. He is nowhere to be found."

"Well, how do you like that?" the professor fumed and stormed back onto the stage.

Looking around at the waiting audience, he grabbed the microphone. "Well, ladies and gentleman, it appears as though Mr. Hestle is running a bit late."

Again, from the corner of his eye, the professor's gaze fell upon the mangled man who was now a little too close to the stage. Two security guards grabbed onto the frightening man and carefully dragged him farther away from the stage.

"Let go! Let go!" the man screamed. He broke free from the guards and ran frantically around the room, screaming in broken English: "He kill me! He kill me!"

As the man got closer to an elderly woman in the audience, she let out a blood-curdling scream as the man continued to rant, clearly pointing at William's picture on the big screen.

"That man! He kill me . . . the jungle! He kill me . . . the jungle!" Blood began to pour from his eyes, ears, and nose as he continued to scream about William.

The audience collectively went into a panic, and then everyone started screaming and running around the room.

But there was one person who wasn't moving

anymore—the mangled monster of a man had passed out in a pool of his own blood.

One of the security guards kneeled to his side and screamed, "Someone call an ambulance—this man is dead!"

Several pairs of soft, feminine hands traveled all over William's body from head to toe, cooling his skin so they could bring his fever down. He brought his hand to his forehead, and it felt as hot as a desert sun. Looking down at his exposed, naked body, he screamed and frantically waved his arms to push the women away.

"What's going on? Where is David?" William looked all around, but he could see his friend nowhere. The only thing he could see with any certainty was a large bonfire in the distance, where several people from the village were gathered, holding hands and chanting.

Suddenly, his head grew heavy, and he lay down in the dirt to relax, the world around him spinning faster and faster. The hands returned, but he didn't have the strength to push them away this time. As the world continued to spin, one woman grabbed his head, while another spooned some awful-tasting soup into his mouth.

"Marianne?" William called. "Marianne, is that you?" If only his girlfriend had come on the trip with them, maybe these strange events wouldn't be happening now. He continued to call out her name while the women tended to William.

He moaned and lifted his head again as his vision started to come back to him. A pulsing pain started at his leg and traveled up his body, and he turned his head to look for the source of the pain. From the top of his knee down to his ankle, his skin had turned blue, and his ankle resembled an overinflated balloon that looked like it was due to pop any second now.

But, as his heartbeat raced faster and faster, something even worse had happened while he was out—somebody had chopped off his foot! He opened his mouth to let out a blood-curdling scream, but he only felt intense pain in his throat . . . and no sound escaped. He tried to breathe through his panic, but he felt his throat begin to close up, and the world suddenly went dark.

William passed out long enough to return to his nightmares.

As William ran through the dark Amazon Rainforest, the frightening noises of the local wildlife taunted him wherever he turned. Hisses, screeches, screams, and growls brushed up against his ears in the dark, but he could neither see an inch in front of him nor an inch behind. He was trapped . . . lost . . . shaking . . . scared . . . until he saw a glowing light appear in front of his eyes. William stopped running and walked carefully toward the light as it glowed brighter and brighter the closer he came.

When he got to the source of the glowing light, he stopped dead in his tracks, and his fear paralyzed him. Staring back at him were two glowing, neon green eyes with a horizontal slit down the middle. He was standing face to face with a venomous snake in the Amazon Rainforest.

As the hands continued to tend to William, his frightened eyes popped wide open as he suddenly remembered how he'd gotten there. He finally found his voice and let out a loud scream that seemed to bounce off every rock, tree, and living thing around him.

When his screams finally stopped, he focused his eyes on the shaman in front of him wearing a long robe made of animal skin and a yellow python skin that hung around his neck. As the shaman moved, William noticed a fringe of large animal teeth on his wrists rattling whenever he moved. William focused on the snakeskin to calm his nerves as it glowed phosphorescently in the firelight.

The shaman's strong hands moved to William's head, and he held him so hard he thought his cheekbones would shatter into a million pieces. Closing his eyes, the shaman chanted in his native language, and with each syllable he spoke, William felt a pulsing pain where his foot should have been. The chanting started out as a low whisper—as did the pain— and it grew louder and louder, eventually echoing for miles throughout the jungle. When William looked all around him, he saw the eyes of the villagers transfixed on the shaman as he inflicted more and more pain. It felt almost unbearable.

When the shaman released William, he grabbed the yellow snakeskin around his neck, stretching it out as wide as he could with his inhumanly long arms. Then the shaman rushed toward the fire, stepping into the middle of the raging flames, stomping on the ground as he resumed his chants. The fire almost seemed to bow to the shaman as he worked his way into a frenzy, chanting louder and stomping into the ground as it shook William to his core.

William opened his mouth to speak, but no words passed through his lips. He tried to move, but he felt paralyzed still. He locked eyes with the shaman suddenly as he walked back through the flames and kneeled down in front of William's mangled leg. Pressing his lips to the wound on his ankle, the shaman sucked the venom from his body, and as he did, the snakeskin in his hands burst into flames. The shaman threw it on the ground and let it burn as he continued to extract the venom from William's ankle.

The people from the shaman's village stood around and watched, the shaman's body vibrating along with the ground underneath him, and William felt as though the entire world would open up and swallow him whole. Then everything suddenly stopped and went eerily quiet. For all William knew, time itself had stopped to make way for the shaman's strange trip into the spiritual realm. As the silence weighed heavily upon his shoulders, the shaman collapsed, and everyone watching gasped.

As seconds seemed to turn into hours, they waited for the shaman to return from the spiritual realm, and William could almost hear it when it happened. A loud buzzing hovered over the shaman's body, growing louder and louder until a strong gust of wind blew through. Once the breeze had disappeared, the shaman stood up slowly, grabbed what was left of the snakeskin, and threw it into the fire. Without looking back or saying a word, he walked off into the distance, leaving the crowd of onlookers whispering amongst themselves.

Then, one by one, they all left until the only thing William could see was a pair of hands tending to his wounds again. The hands forcefully found their way to his lips, and he drank of the toxic-tasting liquid obediently. His body turned numb immediately, and the hands picked him up carefully, placing him softly against a tree. Through his heavy eyelids and blurry vision, he watched his caretaker walk away right before the narcotic drink effect.

William fell back into another memory as he slept.

David leaned across William as the water taxi sped across the river creating white-capped waves. Pointing at some visible smoke plumes above the tall canyon of banyan trees, David said, "Do you think that's the village the committee told us about?"

"It could be," William responded. "There doesn't seem to be any other villages around here. It feels like we're completely isolated out here—like we're visiting the end of the world."

A flock of colorful macaws swooped right over their heads and dove into the branches along the beach ahead of them. He looked down at his watch and said, "It's been about two hours since we left Iquitos, hasn't it?" He looked over at David, who seemed too mesmerized by the scenery to hear him. William raised his voice this time. "I think we're almost there."

The water taxi slowed and pulled over into the shallow water, and then their pilot grabbed their bags and equipment, helping them onto the shore to get settled.

"*Muchas gracias, mi amigo,*" David said as he shook the pilot's hand. "*Recuerda tres semanas—muchas gracias!*"

"Do you think three weeks will be enough time to finish our research?" William splashed water on his face, feeling invigorated by the scenic trip to the middle of nowhere on a small, nameless tributary of the Amazon.

"Well, it will give us a head start, anyway," David responded. "So, we better get our asses in gear so we can finish by the time he returns."

"Great idea! We'll unpack later after we do some exploring," William said, pulling a notebook from one of his packs.

David pulled some dried meat and two large water bottles from his bag, and then started off into the jungle. William followed behind him, stopping occasionally to write down some observations on the way to their destination.

They stopped in front of a large, sparkling waterfall that seemed too picture-perfect to be real. "This will be ideal for our freshwater!" William yelled so David could hear him over the cacophony of buzzing coming from the native insects of the rainforest. He sat next to David on the rocky outcropping as they shared a snack, still staring in awe at the waterfall. "We should keep exploring, though, to see if there's anything closer to camp."

The next two weeks went by in a pleasant blur of foraging and exploring, and they spent their nights by the fire singing Spanish love songs accompanied by the ukelele William had brought with him. After their performance ended, they would each split up the chores, then roll a pair of dice David had carved from a couple of pieces of driftwood they found on the beach to decide on the most-hated chore—laundry.

"Damn. I got laundry again! I think you've rigged these dice somehow," David whined, throwing them across the beach in disgust.

"Don't you worry, *mi amigo*. My time is coming," William said with a laugh.

"It's not funny! I could die out here in this water, you know," David grumbled.

"The snakes are more afraid of you than you are of them," William tried to say with a straight face, but he couldn't stop the laughter from coming.

David just stared at him and looked out on the smooth water for signs of electric eels, sharks, or venomous snakes. "I don't find this very amusing."

On a roll, William had to take one last shot. "What happens in the Amazon stays in the Amazon!"

"You know what, man? I hope I *do* find a viper or a coral snake out here . . . because I'm going to bring him back to see how you like it!"

As their departure date edged closer and closer, they both started to worry they might not find anything worth mentioning upon returning. One evening after the most picturesque sunrise they had seen so far, they headed off for another hike in the vivid raspberry hue cast on them from the sun. After they hiked for hours, William noticed something interesting in the distance. "There's something behind you," William said quietly.

David jumped and ran all around, thinking there might be a poisonous spider or venomous snake in the vicinity. But, when he turned around, he saw exactly what had caught William's attention. They both crept over to a rubber tree and noticed a swarm of insects a short distance away from the tree. Upon closer inspection, they could see no evidence of any insects on the tree's branches.

"That's peculiar," William said. "Why do you think they're not crawling on the tree? I've never seen anything like this!" Upon closer inspection, he noticed something even stranger. He ran his finger along one of the branches, pulling away a thick gelatinous substance. "What in the world do you think *this* is?" He looked expectantly at David, who looked closely at the liquid covering William's finger.

"Why don't we come back tomorrow to study this rubber tree grove?" David asked. "It's much too late to do our research now—we need to hike back to our camp before it gets dark. By the time we get back, it's going to be completely dark."

"I think you're probably right." William pulled out a rag from his pocket and wiped the substance from his hand. "Before we go, though, let's think for a moment about what this could mean for our research. If this turns out to be a natural insecticide, can you imagine what the implications would be? We'll have discovered an insect-repellant rubber tree variety." William looked off into the distance, letting his imagination get away from him. "The magazines, the grants, the applications," he mused. "The fame," he finally whispered quietly to himself.

"What was that?" David asked as he started to get their belongings together.

"Oh, nothing," William said, coming back to reality. "I was just thinking about how amazing it would be if we could replicate this in our lab back at the university. There's so much arsenic in insecticide these days—"

"Yes! No more pollution or destroyed habitats!" David interrupted with excitement.

"Wow! We're going to revolutionize the rubber industry by reducing harmful insecticides, and hopefully, in time, that means we can eliminate the use of arsenic in rubber-tree farming." William's eyes got big, and he started dreaming of his future again.

"We found a brand-new sustainability miracle. You know what that means?" David asked.

"Another $100,000 for each of us, *mi amigo*!" William exclaimed.

"Before we get ahead of ourselves, let's get back to camp. We can return tomorrow to dig up some of the smaller trees to take back to our lab to study closer."

After David and William returned to their campsite, they both enjoyed a lazy meal of fruit and maniac root. But, before it got too late to do their nightly chores safely, William grabbed the dice to see what fate had decided his task should be. "Damn!" he exclaimed.

"Serves you right! You can bet your ass I'll be sitting pretty here on the shore while you endanger your life with a little bit of laundry," David said, smiling as wide as he could.

No big deal, William thought. *We haven't seen a snake out here yet. I'm starting to wonder if we haven't scared them away by now. Piece of cake.*

He picked up his pile of clothes and headed toward the shallow part of the river. On his way to the river, he saw something in the distance that seemed to be moving closer—something that almost looked like it was slithering along the beach. He froze immediately as his fear took over his body. He looked over at the snake, then back to the water, then back at the snake again. It seemed to freeze mid-slither on its way to the river as well.

William's heart raced wildly as both he and the snake stared each other down. "There's only room for one of us in this river," William said, building up his confidence to face the snake.

David watched William carefully from a safe distance, laughing at the turn of events. "Just make a run for it, brother. Remember—he is more afraid of you than you are of him." Already done with the dishes, he leaned back and watched William squirm for his entertainment.

In reality, no one really thought they'd have to face a venomous snake in the Amazon—not until today.

"Oh, this is ridiculous!" William exclaimed. "The bastard doesn't even have legs." With that, he stomped over to the snake to assert his dominance over his domain. But, as he got closer to the snake, the snake still didn't move. It proved to be a showdown of epic proportions.

As William crept closer to the area, his heart nearly leaped right through his chest—and it surged even faster the closer he got to the snake, almost feeling like it might explode entirely. His legs grew heavier, but he forced himself to get closer and closer . . . until . . . upon closer inspection . . . he realized it wasn't a snake at all!

"You've got to be kidding me!" William screamed into the night. He picked up the thick branch and threw it across the beach, David's laughter adding an annoying soundtrack to the event.

"I don't find this very amusing," William mumbled under his breath as he walked back toward the river, stepping a confident first foot into the shallow water.

Suddenly, a sharp pain started right at his ankle, then traveled up his leg. "What the hell?" William exclaimed, looking down at the murky water in enough time to see a water viper remove its fangs from his ankle and slither away through the water. He looked back at David, who still had a smile on his face, completely unaware that William had just been attacked.

"Help! Help!" William yelled. "David! Help! I've been bit!" He looked all around the water, but he couldn't see the snake anywhere. Deserting their clothes in the river, he ran as fast as he could to David who still looked several shades of shocked as everything happened so quickly.

"Jesus!" David yelled. "You were really bit, weren't you?"

"Yeah! And what a great help you are sitting over here in paradise laughing at me!" He tried to push David away, but he felt his body weakening and knew he'd need David's assistance for the rest of their trip. Leaning against his friend, they both made their way up the beach to their tent so William could relax while they figured out what to do.

"Hang in there, old buddy," David said. "We'll

get through tonight and find help first thing in the morning. This snake will not defeat you—you're unstoppable."

These were the last words William heard before he passed out in David's arms. After that, everything turned completely black.

When William looked down at his leg, he saw an area of dead flesh growing as gangrene threatened to destroy more of his leg. He stared at it so long that when he closed his eyes and opened them back up, all he could see was black, rotting flesh everywhere. The image wouldn't leave his mind, and panic began to take over his body. As he continued to sweat profusely and battle what felt like an oncoming heart attack, he screamed for help.

But nobody around him seemed to understand what the word meant. Help would not come for him—only death, decay, and pain. His cries rang out and hit those around him at their core. The shaman rushed to his side to see what had happened.

"Knife . . . knife." William tried to make a cutting motion with his hands to break the language barrier, but the shaman only returned a blank look. For the first time in a long time, desperate tears fell down William's face. He was lost, isolated, and in danger, and the people around him didn't understand how he felt.

The shaman forced some liquid down his throat to calm him, and the natural narcotic began to take effect as the world around him seemed to travel in and out of consciousness. In one of his more sober moments, he saw a hint of hope as he made out the features of a giant pitcher plant nearby. This plant was notorious for being carnivorous and would even digest small rodents if they were unlucky enough to come crawling into their tubular death trap. As he watched insects diving to their death inside the plant, he wondered if there was a way it could help him save his leg.

William crawled over to the plant to inspect the likelihood of this plan, and the tubular structure of the plant appeared exactly large enough to accommodate his slender leg. As he got closer to the plant, some of the men from the village gathered around him and carried him even closer, offering him a prime opportunity to slide his leg inside. "Do you think this will work?" he asked nobody in particular, though the men more than encouraged him. They tied him to the tree with some banyan vines and slid his leg into the tube.

As the cold water from the bottom of the plant

hit William's skin, a shiver ran through his entire body, and he shook like a leaf trapped in a powerful gust of wind. His ankle finally settled at the bottom of the plant, and he felt the dead and dying carcasses of the plant's insect prey rubbing up against his skin and squishing under the weight of his leg. It was an unsettling feeling to give up his fate in the hands of the Amazon Jungle's predatory flora. He didn't relish the fact that he had become just another victim of the monsters created by nature—first the snake and now the pitcher plant.

More than anything, William held a deep, pulsating anger for David, the so-called friend who had deserted him when he most desperately needed him. Somehow, after all this came to an end, he'd find a way to make David pay for becoming a traitor, but now he had to focus on the task at hand.

Staring down at the pitcher plant as the narcotic threatened to plunge him into complete darkness, William felt the plant's digestive juices penetrate his wound, sending unbearable nerve pains pulsating all over his leg. His body reacted by sending tears of pain pouring down his face, and he finally succumbed to the effects of the narcotic as he slipped away into an uncomfortable slumber, twitching, shivering, and shaking as he did so.

Hours later, William woke up to a sharp pain that felt like someone had stabbed his leg repeatedly. As the dark night circled around him, he tried to feel around in the strange liquid he had blindly trusted with his life. Without the benefit of sight, he had to feel around carefully to see what might have caused the sharp pains. He quickly shoved his hands into the cold water, and something wet and furry clawed at his hand, gnashing its teeth wildly. Grabbing onto the creature, he pulled it from the plant and brought it inches from his face.

William let out a blood-curdling scream but felt paralyzed to do much else. Staring back at him were two beady red eyes—the eyes of a dirty, nasty, squealing rat. The rat tried to bite at his face, but he threw it across the jungle and continued to scream for anyone to come to help him. Not to be outdone by only the one rat, he was mortified to learn there were more stuck deep inside the pitcher plant. They swam around like crazy, rabid creatures and gnawed incessantly at his tendons, shredding them into mere ribbons of flesh—only to be digested later by the monstrous pitcher plant.

Panicking, he kicked frantically to get loose from the plant, but the men had tied him so tightly to the tree that he couldn't break free from his tormentor. "Help! Help! Come back! You've made a grave mistake!" Screaming and breathing heavily, he was desperate to run as far away from the plant as possible. He knew if he didn't break free soon, it might be too late for any part of his leg to be saved after this traumatic experience.

As William slipped deeper into madness, he imagined his blood filling the entire pitcher plant, and nobody nearby seemed to care that his life was in danger. "Help! Get me out of here! It's going to kill me!" William screamed so long and so long that his throat burned like someone had lit his mouth on fire.

"David, I'm going to kill you for abandoning me here to die!" William let loose his last attempt for salvation, his anger-filled words bouncing from tree to tree into the jungle that meant to kill him.

After he calmed down and his throat cooled a bit, he suddenly had a short list of people to kill:

The shaman first, for putting me in this monstrous plant to get devoured by rats, then David next, for deserting me in the jungle with no way to escape.

At that moment, William crossed the threshold from human being to monster, his rage ripping through his battered heart and destroying it once and for all. *This is what demons are made of, and I'll make sure they never forget it.*

To distract his mind from the nightmare he'd found himself living in, William stared blankly into the darkness, conjuring up the bitter scene of

David's betrayal only days before the man previously known as William turned into a grotesque clone hell-bent on destroying everyone who had ever caused him any pain.

William opened his eyes, finding himself completely and desperately alone. Looking all around the beach for his traveling companion, he began to panic. "David! David! David? Where are you?"

He looked down at his arms and legs, and he saw that he had been badly burned by the sun. His throat also felt dry, and he knew he'd be in danger if he didn't find help soon. Continuing to call for David, his screams echoed back at him, realizing his friend was never going to respond. Sometime during the night, David had quietly gathered all his belongings and escaped the beach while William lay there unconscious with snake venom traveling all through his body.

"You bastard! You left me here all alone!" William's screams, once again, reached nobody. "He left me here to die," he finally said quietly to himself. "That bastard."

As a breeze blew through the beach, William

also suddenly realized David had taken all his clothes when he deserted him there. As he lay there on the beach with his vulnerability in his hands, the exposed skin on his naked body left him feeling even more lost, alone, and frightened. He didn't know how he was going to pull through this. He needed water. He needed food. He needed medical attention. David had taken all that away from him.

As he tried to stand up, the world started to go fuzzy, spinning and turning until he sat back down on the beach to make the dizziness go away. William got on his hands and knees instead, crawling through the jungle to get to a nearby village where he could find some help—or at least another human being who wouldn't desert him in his time of need.

He crawled and he crawled until he saw a large cloud of smoke rising over the trees, and he knew if he could make it that far, somebody there would be able to help him. William drug himself through the jungle for what felt like hours until he got close enough to the smoke he could almost taste it.

And that was when he finally collapsed. He could crawl no farther.

A group of men rushed to William's side, picking him up and carrying him to a dark hut in the middle of their village. He moaned and groaned as they placed him on the dirt floor—down at the feet of one of the most frightening and respected men in the village, the shaman.

By that time, William's vision had blurred, and the only thing he could see was a large figure cloaked in multi-colored fur. The shaman suddenly woke from a meditative state and turned his attention to the ailing man in front of him. Screaming in a language foreign to William, he dropped to his knees, crawling over to William's leg to inspect his injury. A loud, disturbing, and earth-vibrating laugh escaped through the Shaman's large lips, and the world turned to black.

The shaman. As William's anger about what he had done boiled inside him, he awoke to a group of men untying him from the tree. He wanted to curse and yell at them, only a series of guttural growls escaped. They helped him off the log, and he tried to put his weight on his mangled leg. His legs buckled, and blood gushed from his wounds, a nice parting gift from the pitcher plant that had fed off his leg for the past ten hours.

Looking down at William's destroyed leg, their jaws dropped to see such a monstrosity in front of them. They quickly wrapped his wound with a bandage and argued passionately as they carried him through the jungle. Once they arrived at their destination, they placed William down on the ground and rushed off to find the shaman.

The shaman took his time making his way to William, keeping his unblinking eyes on the injured stranger. He pressed his strong hands onto the wound, and William screamed out, his agony making its mark all over the village. Slowly, the shaman pulled the bandage away and offered no reaction whatsoever to how badly the plant had damaged William's leg. Pulling a satchel of herbs from his pocket, the shaman began to prepare a mixture that would aid William's healing, but William's anger took over then.

"I don't want it! I've had enough of your 'medicine.' I'm leaving!" William tried to speak with his hands to break through the language barrier, but the repulsive sound of his voice distracted both of them. He sounded like a monster from hell—the monster the shaman had created.

"*Necesito algo*. I need something." They both looked at each other blankly because the shaman still didn't understand what William was asking for. "*Serpiente*! A snake! I need a snake." William moved his hands to form an S, and the shaman's eyes finally lit up with understanding.

"I need a snake. Can you get one for me?"

William spoke rapidly, and his eyes darted all around the village as his frantic, nervous energy took over.

The shaman grabbed William's arm and dragged him back through the jungle as William limped alongside him. They both made their way back to the log, and William's anger terrorized his mind to be standing right by the evil pitcher plant again.

William watched carefully as the shaman approached another log several feet away and lifted it from the ground like it was made of air. As he did, a mass of coral snakes sat embedded in the dirt and raised their heads to investigate the intruder.

His first instinct was to scream, but he didn't want to alarm the shaman or the snakes. He had already worked up a brilliant plan, and he didn't want to ruin it by acting like a frightened child.

The shaman bent to pick up a woven basket with his back turned to William. As William crept closer to the shaman undetected, the shaman placed one of the smaller snakes in the basket. Right as he did, William surprised the shaman, pushing him into the mass of coral snakes on the ground. The shaman's screams filled the jungle as they struck his leg over and over.

William knew he had to act fast before the villagers found out who had killed this man, so he grabbed the basket and ran until he found the beach. A familiar tent had been set up close to the shore while he was away getting terrorized by the shaman. Then, in the distance, he saw a familiar face, and he knew he had to be dreaming. There standing in front of him was his long-time girl-friend, Marianne.

He quickly ducked behind the tent so she wouldn't see him; she'd never be able to love a monster like him anyway. After the coast was clear, he hid in the jungle until night fell, when he finally saw David alone by the shore—washing clothes.

William's own words echoed inside his head: *What happens in the Amazon stays in the Amazon*, except he didn't intend it as a joke this time. As he crept closer and closer to David, he held even tighter onto the woven basket that would soon be his murder weapon. Only inches away from David now, he slowly pulled the snake out and raised it above his head.

"I don't think you want to do that."

A deep, accented voice sent out a warning from behind William, and he turned to face the water taxi pilot who had brought them here at the beginning of their trip. His hand shook, and he didn't quite know what to do next. "Please don't get in the middle of this," William begged, eyeing the angry snake that was now baring its fangs. "He deserted me. He left me here to die!" William's screams penetrated the thin fabric on the tent, and he could see someone moving around inside.

"William? William, is that you?" David asked, turning around and approaching William.

William held the snake in David's direction, then in the pilot's. "Stay away from me—both of you! I'll kill you both if you make a move."

The pilot raised his hands and tried to calm William. "Are you sure he left you for dead? I brought him back so he could look for you. You might want to—"

"You're lying!" William screamed. "When I woke up on the beach, I was isolated and alone—dying from a snake bite. I had to find my way to a village so I could find someone to help me. When things got rough, David ran, and I bet he ran right back to collect that grant money without me!"

"No, that's not true! When I woke up, you were gone. You wandered off in delirium at night. I followed your footprints to the jungle, but then lost your trail. I searched the jungle in every direction, but there was no sign of you. I thought . . . I thought you were dead! When I got back to the dorms, I contacted the committee and asked them to use the grant money to start a scholarship in your name. Let's just go back to the city so I can prove it to you," David said, backing farther away from William.

William shook his head and stepped closer to David. "Oh, no. I don't think so. I've made up my mind. You left me to die, so I'm going to do the same thing to you!"

"An eye for an eye? William?" Marianne stepped through the tent opening and out into the dark night.

William grabbed David and spun him around so he could hide behind him, the snake still thrashing in his hands. "Go away, Marianne! I don't want to hurt you."

Marianne didn't retreat; she slowly walked toward William because she knew he wouldn't do anything to harm her. She softened her voice and tried to calm him as she approached. "Since when are you a murderer? We both know you're not going to hurt David. He's done nothing to harm you."

William stepped out in the light of the fire so Marriane could get a good look at his mangled body. "Look at me!" He crept closer and closer to her, not realizing the snake had gotten even angrier than it already was. "Look at me—I'm a monster."

Marianne looked him up and down, and she couldn't hide the shock on her face for long. Tears streamed down her cheeks as she focused on his injured leg. "What happened to you is awful," she finally said quietly, "but it's not David's fault. Let's put the snake down and talk about this." She took one step closer to William, but she didn't realize how close she had gotten.

Before William could move, the snake dug its bared fangs into Marianne's neck, and William was so paralyzed with fear he didn't do anything to help her. The snake continued to attack Marianne, biting her multiple times until she fell to the ground convulsing. The snake then slithered away into the jungle and never returned back to the beach.

David ran to Marianne's side. "What have you done?" he asked, looking back and forth between Marianne and William. "If we don't help her right away, she's going to die!" He lifted her body up and ran toward the jungle while William watched from a distance, shivering, crying, and shaking his head.

He turned back to William and yelled, "What are you waiting for? We need to take her to the village!"

"The shaman . . ." William froze in the middle of the sentence, realizing they'd probably kill him if he ever returned to their village. By now, they probably had discovered the shaman's body in the middle of the jungle.

"Let's go then!" The pilot rushed toward William, grabbing his arm and pulling him into the jungle. "You can take us there."

"It's no use," William finally admitted. "The shaman . . . the shaman . . ."

Two large villagers suddenly appeared along the edge of the jungle with the shaman limping behind them, with one side of his body completely mangled by the snake attack. He pointed at William and spoke quietly to his bodyguards. In response, they lifted their bows and arrows, one pointing his weapon at David and the other pointing his weapon at William.

"Put down," one of the men said in a thick accent gesturing to Marianne's lifeless body.

David complied slowly, then raised his hands in the air. "We don't mean you any harm—we just need to get our friend some help." He pointed down at Marianne who moaned and groaned as her body convulsed.

The shaman's bodyguards kept their weapons trained on the two men as they approached the water taxi. They grabbed the pilot forcefully and hopped into the vehicle, leaving David, William, and Marianne all alone in the jungle.

As David kept his eye on the water taxi disappearing into the horizon, William lunged toward him, grabbing the knife he had sheathed on his belt. He held it up to David's throat and pressed the blade against his skin.

"Look at what you've done!" William burst into tears, and his anger grew even hotter. "Not only did you leave me to die, but now Marianne's going to die too!"

"I promise—"

"Don't you dare speak!" William yelled. "You don't have the right—not anymore." With one fluid movement, William plunged the knife deeper, David's blood coating his face right before he fell to the ground.

After an astounding number of applications have been reviewed by the Committee for Scientific Discoveries, we are pleased to announce that the first annual Danforth Explorer Scholarship has been awarded to Holly Jackson to fund her doctoral research focused on the effects of microdosing mentally ill patients with heliotrope for improved neuroplasticity.

William held this month's issue of *Horticulture Digest* in his hands, and he suddenly felt nauseous at all the implications this announcement held. David hadn't been lying. It seems he did donate all his grant money to create a scholarship, a *Danforth* scholarship at that. He had killed the shaman for nothing. He had killed David for nothing. He had killed Marianne for nothing. With nothing else left to live for, he grabbed the venomous coral snake he had brought back from the jungle out of its aquarium. It hissed and bared its fangs as William brought it closer to his face.

And the last thing he saw before he died were the green, glowing snake eyes from the jungle, and he smiled knowing the nightmare was finally over.

DON'T LET THE BEDBUGS BITE
HUNTER EVANS

Don't Let the Bedbugs Bite

Have you ever been to a haunted house on Halloween? There's one in every town, but you might not believe the stories your friends tell about them. As I drive past the one in my neighborhood, I let out a taunting laugh, and it almost feels as though the house can hear me. With my eyes watching the dark and menacing abode, it appears as though the windows track my every move. Feeling a little creeped out, I turn to my best friend, Lila, who is too busy staring down at her Facebook feed to see it.

I pull my car to the curb and wait for her to look up. "Look at that house," I say, wondering if she's heard the stories too. "It's creepy, right?"

Lila rolls her eyes and looks through me, putting her phone on the dashboard. "Yeah, sure. I guess."

"You think it's haunted?" I laugh before I can get the word out because we both know I don't believe in that crap.

"Yeah, right. So are we going to the mall, or what?" Lila looks away from the house and grabs her phone. "I have a date with Ryan tonight, and I want to buy a new dress." She continues the ever-lasting scroll, and I wonder if she's searching for the secrets to the universe, somehow secretly hidden in an algorithm she can't possibly understand.

"Have you heard the stories about that house?" I whisper, deliberately trying to freak her out. "Jason once told me there's an old witch who's lived there for hundreds of years, and every Halloween, some little kid ends up missing after they try to get inside the house."

"Don't be stupid! Come on, let's get out of here. I've got better things to do today," Lila says.

"I tell you what—you come inside the house with me, then we can go shopping after. I want to see if all the stories are true." Without waiting for her answer, I step outside the car and start running toward the large ornate door on the front porch. I turn back to look, but Lila hasn't moved an inch. I wave at her to get her to follow me, but she shakes her head.

So I guess I'm going in by myself. Typical.

As I step onto the porch, it creaks beneath the

weight of my feet. I stand there frozen, afraid to move, and a black curtain several feet away sways behind the window. Somebody—or something—watches me from the other side. Then my eyes travel to the door, and I see a sign I didn't notice from the road:

CEREUS NIGHT BLOOM PARTY STARTS AT
8:00 P.M.

I look down at my watch and notice it's only five hours away, so I make a mental note and step off the old, rickety porch, slowly backing away with my eye still on the curtain. Glowing red eyes glare back at me, and I turn and run like hell back toward the car.

Without saying a word, I jump back in the car, start it, and speed down the street. A cursory glance over at Lila, and I'm now certain she hasn't stopped looking at her phone for hours.

"See any ghosts?" she asks, looking up at me momentarily.

"I don't know. I did see something, though. I think I'm going to come back later for the cereus blooming party," I say. "Want to come?"

She lets out a deep sigh and puts down her phone. "Did you not hear me tell you earlier I have a date with Ryan? And I wouldn't be caught dead walking into that nasty house anyway."

So it's settled. I'll walk into the witch's lair at 8:00 p.m., and I'll get murdered at 8:01 p.m. *Great plan, Iris.*

Two hours later, I drop Lila off at her apartment to get ready for her date with Ryan, and I head to my place to figure out what one normally wears when they plan to get murdered by a witch. Black jeans. Black t-shirt. Black boots. Yeah, that sounds about right.

Over the next couple of hours, I sit and watch the clock tick down the minutes as I argue with myself about whether or not it's a good idea to attend a bloom party alone at some weirdo's house. Laughing to myself, I realize how ridiculous my thoughts sound. I mean, how dangerous can it be to watch a stupid flower open up? It's probably not going to be all that exciting anyway. I let that thought echo in my mind over and over until I finally look back at the clock and realize it's time to get going.

As I park on the curb next to the house, I notice how much more frightening it looks in the dark. I look up at the porch, then over at my clock. It's 7:55 p.m., and nobody else approaches the front door. But those red eyes appear through the window again, and I feel drawn to them, almost as though I am in a trance. Then, before I lose my nerve, I step out of the car and walk slowly toward the porch. The red eyes seem to glow brighter the closer I get to the steps.

Now standing right outside the door, I raise my fist to knock, but before I can touch the door, it swings wide open, yet nobody stands on the other side of it. Carefully, I peek around the corner, and a long, flowing black dress glides across the floor, almost looking like no person is standing inside it. I want to ask what the hell is going on, but when I open my mouth, I feel too scared to vocalize anything.

Looking back to the front door, I realize I can run like hell to save myself—that is, until the front slams shut, sending vibrations throughout the old house that echo up into my frightened bones. A loud, ungodly scream slips through my lips, and I look around, wondering where that unsettling sound came from. *It came from you, you idiot. Put your head back on.*

When I grab the doorknob, the door suddenly disappears, and I am now fully aware of my entrapment. A voice echoes inside my head that sends the most unsettling pain all through my body:

You have no reason to fear, my child. Just follow the sweet smells if you want to experience the night-blooming cereus. You won't regret it.

The smell the voice tells me about is absolutely intoxicating, and I can no longer think about anything else but following that smell. Its scent is so powerful I can almost see the vapor floating in front of my face, almost like I'm living inside a cartoon. So, like all the characters I remember from my childhood, I follow the smell.

Before I know it, I'm walking down a narrow staircase that's decorated intricately with real spiderwebs . . . with actual spiders living in the webs. I duck and dodge the frightening insects as I walk farther down into my descent into madness. With each step, I imagine myself falling through the rotting wood beneath under my feet, but I manage to make it to the bottom still alive.

It's completely dark down here, but I hear little feet scurrying across the old wooden floor, across my feet, and down the hallway. The little critters seem to be following the sweet floral aroma, too, so at least I won't be alone after all.

Candles light a room just ahead, so I walk into the room, bracing myself for what's about to happen. The darkly ethereal woman in the black dress stands in the middle of the room with about ten children sitting in a circle around her. They are all wearing age-appropriate Halloween costumes that almost seem as though they come from decades past. I wonder if I have managed to travel back in time, but I try not to linger too long on that distracting train of thought.

Welcome, my child. You've arrived just in time.

Slowly, as though time has slowed down exponentially, the flower starts to bloom in the dark room. All the children watch in awe as the white flower opens up to greet them. I notice that something is different about this flower, so I step closer to examine it.

Standing close enough to touch it, I see that the flower is large enough to swallow me whole, and a large amount of blood drips from it, dropping down into a large puddle of blood on the old wooden floor. I touch the flower, and a bit of blood stains my fingertips.

"I've never seen anything like it before," I say, and the woman steps even closer to me. She smells like she's survived a hundred deaths, and I stumble backward to get away from the vile smell oozing from her pores. But there's no fresh air in the room, and I can't quite catch my breath.

"You're the witch," I whisper. "I've heard stories about you."

All the children gasp at my words.

The witch's eyes turn from pale white to blood

red in a flash as she grabs me by my throat. "Do you believe the stories?" she asks, her voice sounding closer to a demon's than a woman's.

"The ghost stories?" I ask, laughing at all those ridiculous tales Jason had told me about the house. "No, I don't believe in any of that. It's all bullshit."

Suddenly, her head falls back, and she lets loose a demonic cackle that makes me feel nauseous. Then she goes quiet and closes the distance between us. "You are a fool," she growls, tightening her grip on my throat.

The floor beneath us begins to shake, and I feel the vibrations moving through my entire body. Next, the room goes completely dark, and a sharp pain enters my throat, hot blood spilling down my clothes and onto the floor. I hear the children's screams pierce my ears, and it feels like blood trickles out and down my ear lobes, periodically dripping down my neck.

Again, her voice enters my mind as the darkness suffocates me:

You will never get out alive.

As the world spins around and around, the children sing around me, their haunting voices lulling me into nightmares worse than this reality.

I can't breathe.

The world is slipping away.

I'm dying.

I must be dying.

I am dead.

Right?

The next thing I know, I wake up on the front lawn of the witch's house late at night wearing different clothes than I remember putting on hours before. I look around for my car, but it's nowhere in sight. Then, reaching in my pocket for my cell phone, I see that it displays a dreaded error message: NO SERVICE.

But I know I paid my bill several days ago.

Without a vehicle, I resign myself to making the two-mile walk home in the dark. When I finally arrive at my house, I see two cars that don't belong to me parked in my driveway like they belong there. *Is this a weird dream—or a nightmare?* Still not catching onto my new reality, I take my keys out and try the lock. No dice.

Then a woman about my age opens the door and stands across from me. In my house? With different furniture? I have to find out what's going on.

She opens the door with caution, asking, "Can I help you?"

"I sure hope so!" I say louder than I intend. "What are you doing in my house?"

The woman looks as confused as I am pissed off. "What do you mean? I've lived here for the past year. Who are you?"

I stumble back on the porch, and she follows me out to the lawn. "Maybe you got the address wrong?" she offers. "Come inside—you can use my phone to call somebody to pick you up. You look like you've had a rough night."

"This can't be happening?" I say, talking to myself, shaking my head. "I was just here yester-day." I look into her eyes, searching for some answers, but we're both at least the same amount of confused about the night's events. "I feel like I'm in a dream—a really bad dream."

"What's your address?" the woman asks. "Maybe I can give you a ride."

"My address is 508 South Baker Boulevard. I've lived here for the past five years." I look up at the number on the house—yep, it still says 508, but I notice immediately that the house has been painted a different color. *Overnight? It can't be.*

Without waiting for her response, I start running down the street as fast as I can. I run through my breathlessness, through my confu-sion, until I'm covered in sweat, standing in front of an all-night convenience store. As I walk through the front doors, I happen to glance down at the newspaper, and I have to look twice:

OCTOBER 30, 2022.

It is almost exactly one year after the night I walked into the witch's house.

I grab the newspaper and walk up to the half-asleep clerk, shoving the offending publication in his face. "What's the date on this newspaper?"

"Why? Are you blind?" the smart-mouthed teenager asks me.

"No, I'm not blind, you idiot! But it's a typo, right?" I ask.

He glances briefly at the date, then back to me. "It says October 30, 2022."

"Yeah? And?"

"And what? The date is correct—it's October 30, 2022, but not for long . . . coz it's almost midnight." He laughs at me and grabs his cell phone.

I let out a deep sigh and push forward. "Do you have a phone I can use?"

He points toward the back of the store, and I head over there to call up Lila. Maybe she can help me make sense of this.

"Whoever this is, it better be good!" Lila answers.

"Is that any way to greet your best friend?" I ask.

"What? Who is this?"

"It's Iris, you idiot!"

"Whoever this is, I don't find this very funny!" With that, she hangs up the phone, and the dial tone screams in my ear.

Well, this just keeps getting weirder and weirder by the second.

I stroll up to the counter, grab the newspaper, and walk out of the convenience store.

"Hey! You have to pay for that," the clerk calls out at me as I walk through the door.

But I don't care. I decide he can put that fifty-cent bill on my tab. So, with the newspaper in hand, I take off to conquer a world that I somehow missed an entire year of. I keep walking until I get too tired to walk anymore. Looking around, I find myself in a park in the neighborhood, and I decide it's as good a place as any to take a much-needed nap. I find the most uncomfortable bed on the planet and curl up to fall asleep, using the newspaper as my unfortunate pillow.

When I awake a few hours later, the sun assaults me with its bright rays, and I grab the newspaper from behind my head. As I'm scanning through the local news, I find a human-interest story toward the back of the newspaper. The headline reads, "A Year after a Local Girl Goes Missing, Family Holds Her Funeral."

But the headline isn't what grabs me by the throat—it's the picture of the missing girl. As I look back into my own black-and-white newspaper eyes, my stomach completely drops, trying to make its way out of my body.

What happened last year that everybody thinks I'm dead? This must be a crazy misunderstanding. There's no way I could be dead . . . right? I'm seriously tired of asking this question!

When I look up, I see an older woman staring me down as she walks by with a grocery cart full of her belongings. She walks over and sits down next to me, periodically looking into my eyes, then away from me. "Your aura is on fire," the woman says. "Why is that?"

I shrug, and tears fall down my face. "Your guess is as good as mine. Maybe it's because I feel like I'm the most lost I've ever been." I don't want to say too much because I'm afraid of scaring another person away from me. Then my curiosity gets the best of me, and I say, "You can see me, right?"

The woman lets out a loud laugh and shakes her head. "Of course, child, I can see you plain as day. What makes you ask that?"

I look all around, then lean in real close to her.

"Because I was thinking I was dead if I'm being honest."

"No, no. You're not dead. Lost? Yes. But not dead." She puts her finger to her lips and looks me up and down. "I see a darkness surrounding you. Yes?"

"I guess you could say that," I say, letting out a sarcastic laugh. "Is it the fact that I slept on a concrete bench overnight?"

"No, not at all. I've spent many a night on that exact bench. I'm speaking of a darkness that someone else has placed on you," the old woman says quietly. "Demonic?" she asks, almost searching my soul to see if I'm possessed. "No, that's not it." She sniffs me for an uncomfortable amount of time. "What I sense in you has more of a witchy vibe. You smell of blood and innocence and fire and death all rolled into one."

"But I am not dead?" I ask.

"Not even close, but you have been cursed," she offers. "I could see her curse on you from a mile away."

"How do you know this?" I ask. Looking deep into her eyes, I see a quick flash of red in her eyes, and it takes my breath away. "Are you her? *The witch?*"

"A witch? Yes. But not *the* witch who did this to you," she explains. "The one who did this was born of rage, violence, and murder. Everything she touches turns bad. She is the one all the good witches fear."

"Alright, so I'm not dead, but I've been cursed by the murder queen herself. Great. What do I do now?" I ask.

The old woman leans into me and whispers, "You must kill her before the full moon comes out. If you wait too long, you will disappear again for another year, doomed to start this whole mess all over again." I look ahead at a tree to take all this new information in, then when I look back for the old woman, she is no longer there.

Leaving the newspaper behind, I walk out of the park and across the street to the cemetery, a chill running up my spine as I walk past grave after grave. Ahead of me, I see a group of unsupervised children sitting in a circle, so I walk over to see what they're up to. As soon I stand behind the group, one of the boys looks up at me with his tired, dead eyes. I suddenly recognize him from the witch's lair.

"It's your first year," the teenage boy says. "You'll get used to it—eventually."

"Oh, yeah? How long did it take you?" I ask, staring at a gnarly scar that extends across his face.

"Only about ten years," he says, shrugging his shoulders like it's business as usual.

A tear rolls down my cheek, thinking about everything I've lost.

"Let me guess—you tried to go home?" he asks.

"I did," I whisper.

The boy looks away from me and back at the ground. "Home doesn't exist anymore. There's just here and there."

"But we're not dead?" I ask.

"Nope," he says. "I've been . . . this . . . for the past thirty years. I feel like a middle-aged man, but somehow, I'm still not."

"You mean, we don't age for an entire year?" I ask.

"No, we only age when we're released from the flower—twenty-four hours at a time. If you think about it, I guess it's kinda cool." He shrugs. "I mean, everybody else wants to live forever, right? I guess we get to—in a way."

I finally resign myself to my new fate, and I sit among the kids as they play jacks. "Have any of you tried to contact your family while you're out?"

A young girl who looked around twelve years old looked up at me. "I did. Once. Do not recommend." Then she looks back down at her game and doesn't say another word.

We stay there playing jacks, marbles, and poker throughout the day and into the night. That is, until the witch calls us back to the basement. A strong urgency suddenly comes over me to follow the kids as they walk back to the dreary house. I figure I might as well follow then since I have nowhere else to go.

It's not like I have much of a choice anyway.

When the darkness disappears, I find myself on my back on the grass again. Presumably, another year has passed, so it's now October 30, 2023. I imagine not much has changed in the past year, so I sit on the lawn and think about what the white witch said to me a year ago.

But how does one kill a powerful witch? I don't know, but I need to at least try. Approaching the house, I step onto the porch, and the wooden slats creak below me much more than they had the first time. I see the witch's red eyes bobbing around inside as she moves from room to room. Then, when I step through the front door, she freezes, looking me over.

"It's too soon! You go away," she hisses at me, throwing some black powder in my face.

I succumb to the darkness again, and I find myself back on the lawn. Apparently, I need to be sneakier about this murder business. Making sure she's not watching me, I crawl across the lawn to get to the side of the house. Right outside the kitchen window, I see a huge pile of rusty knives, as if someone had planted some sort of a murder garden. Being as quiet as I can, I grab one of the old knives and sneak around to the back of the house. I breathe out a sigh of relief to see the grass has grown extremely high—high enough to hide me from her view.

A voice frightens me from behind. "Wanna play hide and seek?" the childlike voice whispers. Turning around, I see a young girl who can't be older than nine or ten years old, and she has that same dark and dreary look as the sad teenage boy from the cemetery.

"Do you think she can see us out here?" I ask.

The little girl shrugs. "I don't know, but I like it out here. I'm all alone out here."

"Well, that doesn't sound like very much fun to me," I reply.

"No, I guess it doesn't."

The girl disappears, and I continue creeping toward the back door. When I reach the door, I put my ear against it, and I can't hear a thing. I figure I have nothing to lose, so I open the door slowly, and staring back at me . . . is the witch again.

Black powder.

Darkness.

This time, I wake up in the park in front of the

same bench I had slept on a year ago. I hear the creaking wheels of the old good witch, and she comes bounding toward me. "Ah, we meet again, child."

I let out a deep sigh and shrug my shoulders. "She's not so easy to kill, you know."

The old lady throws her head back and laughs. "Did you think it would be?"

"Every time I get close to her, she pulls out the black powder—and poof! That's how I ended up here. Is it even possible?" I ask.

The old woman pulls out a small container of white powder. "It is if you have this," she says, putting it in my hands.

"What do I do with it? Snort it like cocaine, or what?"

"You could—eat it, drink it, snort it, shove up your ass. Whatever works for you, child. You just need to consume it somehow," she says.

I grab the container and open it right away. "Okay, here goes nothing."

The woman slaps my hand to stop me. "No! Not right now. This is invisibility powder, but it only lasts for a few minutes—long enough to surprise the black witch so you can kill her. Then, once you get close enough to her, you can stab her, shoot her, strangle her, drown her—however you normally murder people."

"I don't murder people!" I yell louder than I

intend, looking around to make sure nobody heard me. "Let's just say I'm a beginner," I say much quieter.

"All you need is the strength to do it, and you'll find away." The old woman looks down at her watch, then back at me. "But it's starting to get dark. You better hurry up before you get sucked back up into the cursed flower." Then the woman disappears.

Running as fast as I can, I make my way back to the witch's house. Before she can see me, I shove some of the powder in my mouth, letting it dissolve. Right away, I feel my entire body tingle until I can no longer see myself. I want to muse about how badass this witchery is, but I have no time to waste.

Making my way to the backyard, I slide in through the door and watch for a moment as she sets out a row of powers, dried plants, and beakers. *Be strong. You can do this.* I step up behind her and put the knife to her throat, but I've wasted too much time.

The darkness swallows me whole.

The next time I wake up, I feel a new sensation. There is darkness all around me, but I am not outside. Instead, I am trapped inside a small, fragrant dwelling completely alone. I push against the walls, and they seem to move, but they don't move enough for me to escape. That's when I realize it—it is October 30, 2024, but I am still stuck inside the flower.

"Hello? Is anybody in here?" My voice echoes all around, and it's all I can hear passing through my ears for the next several minutes, like an internal, evil voice that knows I can't possibly ever escape this nightmare. Then I hear *her*. She cackles outside the flower to let me know she knows I will kill her if I ever escape again.

I check my pockets, and the white powder is still there, but it does me no good if I can't get out.

"Knock, knock," the witch calls from outside the flower.

I know it's a trap, so I try to ignore her.

"Knock, knock," she screams into the flower, and her voice rips through me as though it could rip through my skin.

"Who's there?" I whisper.

"Ima," she says.

"Ima who?" I humor her.

"Ima never getting out of there alive!" She laughs even louder this time, but as her laugh gets quieter and quieter, I realize she has left the room.

Resigned to my fate as an eternal flower person, I relax against the walls of the flower and close my eyes. Sleep doesn't find me, but at least I know I'm safe in here. The hours pass by, and it feels like years have passed. The only thing I can hear is the thumping of my heart in my chest.

At least I'm still alive.

But it's not much of a consolation prize.

I count the beats for as long as I can, then the darkness takes over as the curse steals another year away from me.

Here I am again—stuck inside this damned flower. As the year-long darkness dissipates, I hear the lost children laughing right outside the plant. I've had an entire year to regain my strength, so I tackle my dilemma with a fighting spirit—quite literally.

Feeling around for anything I can use as a weapon, I feel the sharp edges of the rusty knife I had nearly killed the witch with, and I know exactly what I need to do. I grasp the handle, and I hack away at the flower from inside. Everything around me shakes, but my effort so far isn't enough to gain my freedom.

I keep going, stabbing everywhere I can: above me, below me, beside me . . . everywhere I can think to slice. When my hand gets tired, I relax for a moment, then I start again several minutes later. As I continue to fight my way out of the flower, my tears flow. I'm so close to my freedom I can taste it, but no matter how hard I try, it feels like it's not ever going to be enough.

And the bugs. *Lord, the bugs!* This damn flower is invested with bugs. It has been my bed for 364 days of the year, and my bed has these disgusting bugs crawling all around inside it and on me.

Finally drained of all my energy, I give up the fight. I wait . . . and I wait . . . and I wait for the children to return, but they never come back. The year-long darkness never returns, either, and I think I must have done something to change the course of events.

"Hello? Is anyone out there?"

Nobody answers—not even the black witch. It's just me and my eternal thoughts, waiting for someone to save me—somehow. I have no concept of time while I'm in here, but years must have gone by while I wait for some miracle to come set me free.

But it never comes.

The only thing that rescues me is time itself.

Then, one day, the plant finally ejects me out into the dark night, but when I look behind, I am amazed to see that the witch's house is no longer standing. Standing up, I look around to see that the only thing around me is an empty field with rows upon rows of night-blooming cereus. Mesmerized by their beauty still, I watch in awe as their lovely petals make their way out into the moonlight.

A car pulls up next to the field, interrupting my flower gazing. I watch as a middle-aged man approaches me and extends his hand to shake mine. "My name is Austin Black," the man says. "I've been coming here for the past thirty years in hopes of finding you again."

I study his face closely and see a familiar scar across his cheek—this is the teenage boy who told me I could never go home again. "You escaped . . . but how?"

"You set me free," he says, tears welling up in his eyes. "I know it was an accident, but I truly am grateful for what you did for me—for all of us."

"The others? They survived?" I ask, a little hope spring up inside me.

"Well, they got out," he said, a familiar frown plaguing his face. "But the rest of them died— mostly by drug overdose or suicide. The black witch left her mark, and they couldn't handle the trauma."

"Oh," I say, "well, at least you got out. You survived. That's something."

"I did," he says, "and you can too."

Austin goes to his car's trunk and returns with an arsenal of garden tools. He throws them down on the ground and looks at me. "This year we are going to kill this plant before it consumes you again!"

We both start hacking away at the enormous plant. I start by testing the waters, cutting off one leaf at a time, but another one magically grows back in its place. "Maybe we should start with the roots."

I get on my hands and knees and pull the dirt away with my hands, trying to locate the roots. They are thick and black, and when I touch them, they feel hot, and they seem to have a heartbeat that pulses against my fingertips. "This damned thing is going to fight back," I mumble under my breath. I realize that if the plant has a pulse, then it most certainly has a heart.

"Austin, help me dig over here! I'm trying to find the heart, and I think I'm close," I say, checking each root. With each one I touch, the pulse beats stronger.

"Plants don't . . ." Austin starts to say.

"Well, this one does!" I yell. "Keep digging!"

The closer I get to finding the center of the root system, the more the plant moves its branches. It wraps around my arms to prevent me from going farther, but before I have time to tear them away from me, Austin keeps cutting them away from my body. We keep moving like this until I find a large black bulb entangled in its complex root structure. As I hold the bulb in my hands, it beats wildly. I squeeze hard, but it continues to beat.

"Austin! Over here! Get this bastard!" I place the bulb on the ground, and he pulls back with a large ax and splits the bulb in half, nearly taking my foot along with it.

We all back away from the large plant as it falls to the ground, twisting and turning in every direction. It spurts out a thick black liquid as it moves around, then it stops suddenly, the world goes terrifyingly quiet.

Too quiet.

I feel a slight rumbling underneath my feet. "Run!" I scream as I take off running myself. I do not want to be anywhere near this thing whenever it does what it's about to do. Finally safe on the pavement, we stand by Austin's car as we watch the ground open wide, pulling the mother cereus plant with it—and all its little creepy babies. The dirt in the field spins and spins around, pulling every last petal, leaf, root, and branch with it.

Then, as the sun starts to rise, everything finally calms down. I look over at Austin and realize we both must look like we've been through a war zone. Austin has several cuts and bruises all over his body. I collapse against him, and I feel tired for the first time in a long time. It plagues me so deeply it hurts, but I welcome the feeling of being entirely human again. I'll take the pain and the wrinkles over the nightmare I experienced any day.

Two days later, I wake up in Austin's guest room, feeling like a brand-new person. I smell the bacon cooking and the coffee brewing. Before I step out into the living room to join him for breakfast, I step in front of the mirror, not entirely prepared for what I'm about to see.

I stare back at my youthful face, and it almost feels like all of this was only a nightmare. My face looks as smooth as it did the day I first stepped into the black witch's house. I touch all the angles of my soft skin, unable to believe what's looking back at me.

Haunted houses? Yeah, I'm still pretty skeptical. But I'll walk 100 miles out of my way to avoid a witch—good or bad, that's someone I never want to mess with again in my life. And when I go to bed each night, I will check to make damn sure there are no bedbugs in it.

BERMUDA TRIANGLE

HUNTER EVANS

Bermuda Triangle

When Alexis looked down at the digital clock on the instrument panel, she knew the time had to be wrong. The clock read 1:24 p.m., but as she looked at the dark sky ahead that threatened to swallow her small plane, she shook her head in disgust and tried to concentrate on the task at hand. Only an hour ago when she left the airport in sunny Fort Lauderdale, it had been so bright she could hardly see in front of her.

Looking down at the picture on the empty seat next to her, she focused on why she had left in such a rush in the first place. Someone had spotted Howard Blake, a renegade Air Force pilot, off the shores of The Bahamas, and the reward for bringing him back to the States was too high to ignore.

Focusing back on the treacherous terrain

ahead, she wiped at her tired eyes to get rid of the deceitful images her mind displayed. Ahead, a dark, gigantic cloud spun around like an F5 tornado, and she knew that didn't track with the reading she saw on the anemometer—the wind wasn't moving fast enough to produce such an anomaly.

It must be sleep deprivation, she reassured herself, pushing forward to her destination. But, as she got closer, the large funnel cloud seemed to grow exponentially, and it shook her small aircraft more than she had ever experienced in her two decades as an amateur pilot. *You're just seeing things, Alexis. You need to keep going.*

Ten years before Alexis set off on her mission, Howard Blake's face got plastered all over the news after a failed rescue mission he led off the coast of Florida when the USS Oriskany sent out a distress signal, then was never heard from again. The last thing the world heard from Howard Blake was a call for help on his trip back to Florida after he discovered everyone on board the ship had disappeared "into thin air," according to Blake.

When Blake didn't land at the closest Air Force

base within the next twenty-four hours, the entire nation sat on the edge of their seats when multiple failed rescue missions came back with no news of Blake or the USS Oriskany. Then months passed with no word—and then it was years.

Alexis had heard about his disappearance, of course, but his story never interested her until she received a call in the middle of the night, right after midnight on Halloween—the night she took off from Fort Lauderdale. The voice on the other end of the line announced himself as "The Night Flyer," and Alexis laughed through most of the call, thinking it was some sort of Halloween prank.

"I assure you this is not a joke," the deep voice had announced, "and if you come back with the prize, I'll pay you a finder's fee of $500,000."

"What's the catch?" Alexis asked. "This sounds too good to be true."

"There is no catch. If you fly out to The Bahamas and bring Howard Blake to me, you'll be half a million dollars richer. And, as a sign of good faith, I've already wired you 20% of that fee to cover any expenses you might incur on your trip."

Before she responded to this ridiculous information, she pulled out her cell phone as The Night Flyer went over the details. When she signed into her checking account, the results had left her speechless. The last time she checked her account, she had a whopping $6.14 in her account. But now

. . . an astounding number stared back at her—it was exactly $100,006.14.

This was not a joke.

She had never seen that much money in her entire life.

The darkness continued to swirl around Alexis, and it spun her plane around like it was a child's toy. She grabbed her radio, but all the electronics lost power. With nobody to call for help, Alexis found herself completely alone in a situation she wasn't trained to handle. As the plane continued to spin around, Alexis had a hard time keeping her balance, but she needed to find a way out of the plane before it split her in two.

As the plane tossed her around like a rag doll, she looked around for her parachute so she could jump safely. She knew she might not survive, but it was the only chance she had. After she finally got it on her back, she opened the cargo door and looked down at the blackness running underneath the plane.

Jump, she encouraged herself, but she never got the chance to. Some unknown force inside the plane pushed against her back, sending her falling through the dark air. The turbulence pulled at her body and knocked her around until her head finally knocked against the solid steel of her airplane. But, instead of her entire world going black, all she could see was white as a blinding light engulfed her.

A witness spotted Howard Blake off the coast of The Bahamas two days ago, and several rescue missions have come back empty-handed. The Air Force wants to keep this information quiet until Blake can be brought back home. This is why your complete discretion is key to a successful mission.

Still stuck in a world full of blinding light, as an unknown male voice read these words out loud, she recognized them immediately—they were the exact instructions she had received from The Night Flyer less than forty-eight hours ago. Alexis fought against the light to find the source of the voice. Finally, she blinked her eyes open, and saw a large, muscular, tanned man in a green t-shirt standing on the other side of the room.

She looked past the man through a window that told her she had landed somewhere tropical. After she struggled to sit up, she turned around to get a better view of her surroundings—and she saw turbulent ocean waves that seemed to go on forever.   As the memories of the plane crash swirled around in her mind, she groaned out loud when she remembered her plan had gotten destroyed in the . . . tornado? In the Bahamas? *That can't be right.*

Hearing her stir in the hospital bed, the man walked over to Alexis with an angry look on his face. "Explain yourself," he practically growled, still holding the offending folder in his hand. "What do you want with me?"

She looked from the water to Blake, shaking her head. "You're him?"

Reluctantly, he shot his hand forward to shake hers. "Howard Blake—yes."

Alexis cringed as Blake nearly crushed her hand. "Someone contacted me last night to come to find you. The world's been looking for you ever since you disappeared. And you've just been in the Bahamas? All this time?"

Blake's loud laugh seemed to vibrate the entire room, matching his enormous presence. "What makes you think you're in the Bahamas?"

"I'm not?" Alexis asked. Ok, *now*, she was completely confused. Had she veered off course somehow? She shook her head, and then asked, "Where in the hell am I?"

Blake set the file down on her bed, and then

walked around the room, pointing out the terrain beyond them. "Welcome to the Bermuda Triangle, my friend. *This* is where I've been for the past decade—not the Bahamas." Realizing she might need a moment alone, Blake left the room, locking her door from the outside.

Alexis limped over to the door, pounding as hard as she could. "Wait! You can't just leave me here. Let me out!" She continued to beat her fists against the door, but Blake had already left. Her screams simply echoed down the hallway.

She looked back to the window. Everything looked foreign to her and she suddenly felt more lost and useless than she ever had in her life. She tried to open the window to escape that way, but she realized she was stuck in the room for the foreseeable future.

The Bermuda Triangle? Really? Blake must have hit his head hard if that's where he thinks he is. This mission is going to be much harder than I thought.

A knock sounded against the door, interrupting Alexis's thoughts. "I'd let you in, but I'm trapped in this damned room!"

Blake unlocked the door and stepped back into the room, raising his hands over his head in surrender. "Calm down, Alexis. It was just for a few minutes! Are you ok to walk?"

"I might be a little slow, but I can make it," Alexis said.

Blake led her down the dark hallway, then outside the building. Sweat almost immediately formed all over her body as she stepped under the blaring sun. She tried wiping her face clean, but more sweat took its place.

"Where's my plane?" she asked, stepping into the little bit of shade she could find.

"I can take you to it, but I'm afraid it's beyond repair," Blake replied. "And, even if you did find a way to fix it, you won't find it easy to leave this island."

"I've taken off in worse conditions—I assure you," Alexis said.

Blake shook his head, laughing softly. "You don't believe me."

"Well, what's so special about this island, then?" Alexis asked.

"Nobody's even been able to leave—at least not when the triangle beacon is blocked." He led Alexis out of the shade and pointed up at the sky. "Look up there and tell me what you see."

Alexis tried to look, but the entire sky seemed to be engulfed in a blinding, white light. She quickly looked away and covered her eyes. "I can't —it's too bright."

"Well, once every ten years, the beacon opens up, and the sky turns the most amazing blue you've ever seen. But can you guess when the last time I saw that amazing blue sky?" Blake asked.

Alexis shook her head.

"Last night, my friend. I'm afraid you're stuck here for a long time," he said. "But you still want to try—I can tell."

Alexis let out a deep sigh. "I do."

"Alright. Well, I'll take you to your plane tomorrow. You need to get some rest first," Blake said, leading her back inside the air-conditioned building.

The next morning, Alexis awoke to a loud knock on her door. When she didn't answer right away, the knocking continued until she made it to the door to open it. Blake stood on the other side of the door with a large food cart containing every type of breakfast food she could imagine.

"Eat as much as you can before we head out—you need as much fuel as you can get. The heat here in the triangle burns it off faster than you'd think," Blake said, pushing the cart next to the bed. He pushed a chair next to the cart and pulled out two large plates so they could eat breakfast together.

"Just how far away is my plane?" Alexis sat

down on the bed and piled an array of food on her plate.

"It's about a two-mile hike from here," Blake said.

"Damn. I was hoping you'd have a car or something to take us there," Alexis replied.

Blake laughed, and then said, "Our technology here is quite limited, but I'm hoping to change that soon."

"How so?" Alexis asked.

"Hurry up and eat. I'll tell you on the way." Blake stood up and looked out the window, then walked over to the counter and flipped through the file contents again.

Once they started their hike, Blake carefully explained his plan. "Don't laugh at me," he started, "but I think I've found Atlantis."

Alexis stopped walking abruptly, laughing. "You what?"

"It's not as far-fetched as you think! You're actually on Bimini Island, which has a large man-made structure submerged off the coast the natives call Bimini Road, thought to have been created by the people of Atlantis," Blake explained. "I've been working on excavating it for the past five years, and I think I'm close to making contact."

"Making contact with whom?" Alexis asked

though she was afraid of what the answer might be.

"The people of Atlantis," Blake answered.

"Oh, I see." Alexis looked off in the distance, wanting to talk about anything but the myth of Atlantis. When she did, she saw smoke still billowing from her airplane, and she took off running to survey the damage.

"I'll come to check on you later," Blake called, but Alexis had run too far away to hear him. He shook his head and turned around to go on his adventure.

Once Alexis got a few feet from her airplane, she bent over to catch her breath. The sun felt much more scorching than it had the day before, and it had drained her energy rather quickly, just like Blake had warned her. Looking back at her plane, she saw the sun glimmering off every surface. Not thinking, she touched the metal surface, and smoke poured from her finger as bubbles formed on her fingertips. It would be a bit tricky to fix her airplane if she couldn't touch it, so she looked around for a rag or some gloves inside the cockpit.

Pulling out an old grease rag from the front of the plane, she inspected every inch on the outside of it, looking for any anomalies that might prevent her from taking off. As hard as she looked, she didn't find one blemish on the outside of the airplane. Looking over it, if she hadn't known she'd crashed, she wouldn't be able to tell anything was wrong with it.

Jumping back inside, she surveyed the instrument panel. Nothing seemed cracked or damaged, but it seemed as though it was dead to the world anyway. She pulled a screwdriver from a toolbox in the plane and began taking the panel apart. Once inside, she noticed all the wires looked pristine—exactly as they should because she always took great care of her equipment.

"I don't know what I'm going to do," she moaned to herself. "I can't be stuck on this island with a lunatic who believes in fairy tales and unicorns!" Then she laughed, realizing the pure insanity of it all. *The Bermuda Triangle. The Lost City of Atlantis. If I'm dreaming, this is a straight-up nightmare!*

Suddenly, a large prehistoric-looking bird flew into the windshield and fell onto the ground. She jumped out of the plane and ran to see what had happened. It looked up at her with the most beautiful violet eyes, and then suddenly stopped moving. The bird had died. Pulling the old rag from her back pocket, she wrapped its body as best as she could and laid it in the back of her plane. Once she returned home to Florida, she could have someone look into exactly what kind of bird it was.

Hoping and praying for a miracle, Alexis went back to try the ignition. The first time she turned it, nothing at all happened. Then, when she turned it a second time, a huge spark ignited, and black smoke poured out of the instrument panel. If she had any hope of getting out of here before, she certainly didn't now. With her instrument panel on fire, she'd need a direct act of God to find her way back home.

Getting out of the plane, she walked around to the propellor at the front and stared long and hard at the blades. With the sleeve of her shirt, she grabbed onto one of the blades and tried to spin it, but it wouldn't budge. Not long after that, the wheels of her plane suddenly deflated, having been melted by the blaring sun she was certain came from the devil himself.

"What's wrong with you?" she whispered out loud, staring desperately at the plane in front of her. "I know we had a rough trip, but I can't find anything wrong with you!"

"Frustrating, isn't it?" Blake called from right behind Alexis, scaring the hell out of her. "I spent about a year trying to fix my plane, but no matter what I did, it still wouldn't work. All the while, people kept telling me it was no use. I guess I should have listened."

"I, too, have a problem doing what's good for me. If you came to talk some sense into me, you're wasting your breath. I'm afraid it can't be done," Alexis said, still staring ahead at her dead plane. "I suppose that's why I felt like I had to take this job."

"What do you mean?" Blake asked.

"I know it sounds about as unreal as landing in the Bermuda Triangle, but some man by the name of The Dark Flyer set this all in motion. He must have known how dire my financial situation was because he transferred a six-figure advance to my check account to come to look for you," Alexis said. "But I guess money doesn't matter when you're stuck on a tropical island with no way to escape."

Blake laughed and shook his head. "The Dark Flyer, you say? Sounds like a superhero name."

"Or maybe a villain," she said, laughing along with Blake.

"Come back with me? The humidity has calmed down a bit. I'll show you around the island," Blake offered.

Alexis looked up at the plane, then back to Blake, shrugging her shoulders. "Might as well. This piece of junk isn't going anywhere today."

"Let me guess: the instrument panel caught on fire?" Blake asked, leading the way away from the plane wreckage.

Alexis nodded her head reluctantly.

"Mine too. One of these days, you're going to

believe me. I'm telling you—this island hates technology of any kind," Blake said.

They walked for a mile north until they came to a village. Alexis saw shops, markets, and people walking up and down the dirt road they walked down. They all smiled and waved at them as they passed, excited to see another new resident of Bimini.

"This is our downtown area. I remember thinking it looked like the Wild West when I first arrived. I barely recall how strange this all felt those many years ago." Blake stepped onto the dirt sidewalk and opened the door to the Bimini library.

Alexis surveyed the shelves of books, noting they looked much different than the books back home. "Are these all handwritten?" She picked up one of the books and flipped through its pages. The book looked to be handwritten in a thick long-lasting ink she figured was probably handmade by one of the Bimini residents. As she ran her hand over the letters, she could feel the ridges of the letters brush against her fingertips.

"Yep. As I said, we have no technology here, so everything you see was made by someone's hands. You won't find any Hemingway or Shakespeare here—unless, of course, somebody rewrote it from memory," Blake explained.

When they returned to Blake's compound, an

entire crowd of men had been waiting on him to return. The strongest man stood drenched in ocean water holding a diamond larger than Alexis had ever seen. It seemed to sparkle at every angle, like some magic stone sent from the heavens above.

"We've broken through to the diamond crust," the man said, hardly able to speak through his breathlessness. "The entire interior of the wall is made up of this material."

"It looks like a diamond," Alexis whispered in amazement.

Blake grabbed the large jewel and turned it over in his hands. "It does, indeed. Let's take it inside and inspect it." Blake walked through the front door, and lights suddenly appeared from nowhere. The room looked as though it was lit by 100 lamps, but there were no lightbulbs to be found anywhere. He stopped, looking up at the ceiling. "Well, that's new." Then he turned to one of the men and asked, "You ever see that happen before?"

The man shook his head; nobody had ever seen that happen.

They all followed Blake to his garage, and he pulled out a large magnifying glass, then placed the stone underneath it. When he looked through, he saw tiny organisms swimming around inside, almost like an entire ocean existed inside the diamond-like crystal.

He turned to the crowd, saying, "What else do you think it does?" He pulled out an old digital clock from his drawer and placed it next to the stone. The red digits suddenly sprang to life and turned until they landed at the right time. Blake laughed out of surprise and delight, turning to Alexis. "Do you know what this means?"

She shook her head; she was as confused as everybody else.

"It means . . . for the first time in history, Bimini finally has electricity!" Blake exclaimed.

"Too bad our instrument panels already blew up," Alexis said, "or we could get the hell off this island."

"Don't give up just yet, my friend. There has to be a way to get you back home—if that's what you want to do," Blake said.

Over the next few hours, Blake performed several experiments with the diamond, but its energy never waned. If anything, it grew more powerful the longer he worked with it. Alexis eventually got bored of watching him play around with it, and then went back to her room to go to sleep for the night.

When Alexis woke up the next morning, the compound felt unnaturally quiet. She walked from room to room to find Blake, but he was nowhere to be found. Finally giving up her search for him, she walked into the kitchen to find something to eat. On the counter, she found a note Blake had left her:

Dear Alexis,

I've gone back to Bimini Road to explore a bit today. Take some time to relax, and I'll be back by nightfall. If you change your mind, though, here's a map of where I'm headed. Our location shouldn't be too hard to find if you're feeling adventurous.

See you soon,
Howard Blake

Alexis let out a deep sigh and looked around the room. After eating several pieces of fruit and drinking a glass of milk, she grabbed the letter containing the map and stepped outside to start on her journey.

An hour later, she finally hit the part of the shore that led to Bimini Road, and she looked across the water for any signs of movement. After several minutes of looking, she finally saw Blake's head pop out onto a wooden platform on the water, and she ran to meet him to see if he'd discovered anything more.

"You made it! Excellent!" Blake pulled her onto the platform and led her over to the tunnel where they were working inside. "Look down here—that's where we've been all morning."

When Alexis looked down, she saw a wide tunnel that looked to have a thick wall made up of the exact material the stone had been made of. As far as she could see, the wall was thick, sparkling, and magical. "Where does that lead?"

"There's a large door down at the bottom, but we haven't gained entry yet." Blake helped Alexis down into the tunnel, guiding her down the wooden ladder they had made. He climbed in after her and followed as she slowly made her way to the bottom.

When they both got to the bottom, an orange light emitted from behind the large door, and a dark figure appeared behind it. His skin was covered in black scales, and all his features were also black, making him look almost like an underwater demon. A blue light shot out from behind his black eyes, and the door popped open.

All their hearts raced simultaneously as the creature looked directly at them, and a wave of anxiety swept across their group. Alexis grabbed her chest and backed away until his gaze fell to the ground.

"You are entering the City of Atlantis." His voice sounded soft and ethereal—not as menacing as he looked.

Alexis looked back at Blake, and her eyes grew exponentially. "This can't be real," she whispered.

Blake only looked back at her; the creature had rendered him speechless.

"Follow me," the creature said.

They all stepped through the doorway, following the mysterious creature as they walked through Atlantis. Alexis tried pinching herself as they continued walking, sure she'd be waking up any time now. But it wasn't a dream—this was real. She simply couldn't believe her eyes.

Everything around them glistened and looked out of this world. They saw gadgets they'd never seen before—things still waiting to be invented on Earth. Bright lights illuminated their surroundings, and it almost looked as though they were walking inside a rainbow.

The creature turned down several brightly lit hallways until they came to a dark door. Then he turned to them and said, "Wait here for King Ellexon." When Alexis turned to look at him, the creature turned into a hologram and disappeared. She felt as though she was watching an episode of *Star Trek.*

Moments later, the door swung open, and a large man with pastel green skin greeted them at the door. "Welcome to Atlantis!" His voice boomed as though it were powered by a megaphone. His inhumanly white teeth sparkled behind his wide smile as he turned and led them further into his chambers.

"Forgive Alejou. It has been quite some time since any of our people have seen your kind," the king said, sitting in his oversized chair that glistened with emeralds, rubies, and all colors of diamonds. "I assume you've broken down our protective wall for a reason." The king waited for someone to speak, but nobody could find the words. "What is it?"

Alexis pushed Blake, and he stumbled forward.

"Uh . . . King Ellexon? Thank you for your kindness. We are from a place called the Island of Bimini, where people from outside the triangle have mysteriously disappeared to with no way of escaping," Blake explained. "We've heard legends of your city for decades, but nobody has ever believed you to exist."

King Ellexon's laugh covered the room like a

thick blanket. "I assure you—I am quite real!" He looked around at the group of humans staring back at him. "I understand your predicament. Bimini Island wears the Coat of Atlantis. It is a protective shield that keeps our city safe from intruders. We've been trying to seal the beacon, and we were close—that is until your pilot arrived here this week."

Alexis tried to back away from the group, but Blake pulled her forward.

"No, no, no!" The king laughed, a little softer this time. "It is quite alright. But, I can assure you, after she gained entrance through the beacon, it will no longer open for new visitors or anyone who wants to escape. The Coat of Atlantis is what's responsible for the treacherous waters that prevent any boats from escaping—and for the death of technology all around you."

"So . . . I . . . I . . . am stuck here . . . forever?" Alexis stumbled over her words, feeling shy for the first time in her life.

"Not exactly," the king offered. "I can provide you passage back to the shores of Florida where you came from, but it is a one-time offer, I am afraid. We are readying our submarine, and we will take you all outside the triangle once it's ready."

"All of us?" Blake asked. "But what if we want to stay?" Blake had gotten used to life on Bimini

Island, and he couldn't stand the thought of returning to civilization.

"No choice, I'm afraid, young man. As we speak my people are building another shield to protect us from any other intruders, so you won't be able to leave the way you came." King Ellexon stood up abruptly as Alejou walked into the room. "Is it ready?" he asked.

"It is, Your Highness," Alejou responded, bowing at his king.

Right then, two other workers appeared in the room and escorted them out. They led them onto the submarine, quickly pre-programmed it as the engine sprang to life, and exited immediately. The submarine raced through the water with only them onboard.

They sat in silence for the whole voyage, still amazed at how the events had played out. Before long, the submarine rose to the surface and came to a complete stop on the shores of Florida at Fort Lauderdale Beach. Alexis was the first to step out, grateful to be back home.

Now, her only question was what to do about Blake. Turn him over to The Night Flyer and claim the rest of her finder's fee? With that reward money, she'd be so rich; she could retire early!

"Retire early," Alexis said sleepily, as she stretched languorously.

Suddenly she bolted upright in bed and grabbed her phone off the nightstand next to her.

"April 2nd? Wait, what? I have been sleeping all day? That medicine the doctor gave me for my migraine must have been stronger than I thought!"

Alexis popped out of bed and realized she was famished. After making herself a huge plate of food and an even bigger cup of tea, she headed to her computer to log on.

"Must have all just been a dream," she muttered to herself as her bank account information loaded onto the screen.

When she saw the hefty $500,000 recent deposit, she let out a scream as her eyes popped out.

"A dream . . . or was it?"

About the Author

Hunter Evans is an award-winning author who writes horror, paranormal, and fantasy works. He has a small home business which caters to the legal profession and enjoys gardening and traveling.

Also by Hunter Evans

Don't Let the Bedbugs Bite

Bermuda Triangle

Snakes Eyes Collection of Horror Shorts

www.ingramcontent.com/pod-product-compliance
Lightning Source LLC
Chambersburg PA
CBHW061328120726
48001CB00002B/741